C000224731

Tales from the Parish
31 short stories

Stefania Hartley

THE ✳ SICILIAN ✳ MAMA

ALSO AVAILABLE AS
EBOOK AND LARGE PRINT
BOOK

Copyright © 2022 Stefania
Hartley

ISBN: 978-1-914606-13-7

Stefania Hartley asserts the moral
right to be identified as the author
of this work.

This is a work of fiction. Names,
characters and events are solely
the product of the author's
imagination.

Stories 1 to 17 and 19 to 31 were
first published in The People's
Friend magazine.
Cover illustration and design by
Joseph Witchall
https://josephwitchall.com/

To my town

CONTENTS

1. HENS FOR FATHER

His parishioners were his "flock", all right, but sometimes Father Emmanuel Okoli wished he had a literal flock, too. Keeping sheep and lambs in the presbytery's garden would be pushing it a bit too far even in a country parish like his, but he reckoned a small flock of hens would do just right. Back home in Nigeria, every family in the village kept hens and hardly anyone bought eggs.

Sometimes he missed home, but he'd made a decision as a student in the Irish mission school that one day he would give back what he had received. When he became a priest, he asked to go to Ireland and, from there, he was posted to a village in the Cotswolds.

As he waited for the kettle to boil, Father gazed out of the window. There was enough space in the back garden for a few hens, but the lawn would be wrecked. And the neighbours might not be happy. But if he kept hens, he wouldn't have to buy eggs. He might even have enough to give away as gifts when he was invited out to dinner, and could give some to the neighbours, too.

But a coop and a run were expensive, and the fence would need to be tall and sturdy to keep away foxes. They weren't expenses he could afford now. He stopped daydreaming, finished his breakfast and went upstairs to get dressed for his meeting with the bishop.

He hadn't really given this meeting much thought. If anything, he had looked forward to it. He had an idea of asking the bishop if he could study for a PhD in Canon Law.

But when he got there and the bishop avoided eye contact, Father Okoli began to feel nervous. Was it bad news? He felt a hot rush of blood to his cheeks.

"Hello, Emmanuel, how are you?"

"Very well, thank you." Father Okoli sounded unconvincing even to himself.

"How are things in the parishes?"

Ah! A parishioner must have complained. He couldn't think of anything overly controversial in his sermons, so perhaps they were just boring. But boring sermons wasn't a serious enough offence to be reported to the bishop. He sighed. "Very good, thanks."

The bishop shifted on his seat. It was

obvious he had something difficult to say and that Father's short answers were making his job harder. "I was a bit worried about saying this to you, but I really have no choice…"

Father swallowed hard. Childhood memories of headmasters' offices resurfaced.

"This year three priests have retired and one has passed away, leaving five parishes uncovered. I know you already have Harleywood and Oldwell and I wouldn't have burdened you with a third one, but you're one of our youngest priests and you're the closest to Moreton-on-the-Edge. What are your thoughts?"

Father's immediate thoughts were "Goodbye, PhD" and "Goodbye, hens". The extra work of yet another flock of people would barely give him time to breathe, let alone study or look after livestock.

But his relief at not being in trouble with the bishop or the neighbours or the parishioners was so big that he grinned. His parishioners didn't hate his sermons after all. The bishop must have interpreted his grin as a sign of approval because he smiled with relief.

"Great. I knew I could count on you, Emmanuel!"

And that was how it happened. Father Okoli got Moreton-on-the-Edge.

The following day, he went on a recce of his new parish with obedient resignation. An affable parish administrator called Belinda showed him around the church and the presbytery. They were old but well looked after.

However, as they approached the back garden, Belinda suddenly looked a little nervous. "I hope you don't mind, Father…I've taken care of them lately and I can continue to, if you want."

She opened the gate and there, before Father Okoli's eyes, stood a beautiful chicken run, full of hens who clucked cheerfully at their new master. Divine intervention!

☐

2. THE CHEESE RACE

Being entrusted with a third parish hadn't turned out to be as bad as Father Okoli had feared, and it had come with a parish administrator to assist him. Belinda Clarke had already proved herself an invaluable help with the parish office paperwork, also providing hen-keeping tips and shedding light into the life of his new home, Moreton-on-the-Edge.

"Next month is the cheese race," Belinda told him one morning. "If you want to make friends and know who's who in the village, you've got to go."

Father always liked a challenge, and making friends even more. Also, he loved cheese, and hoped that the prize would include a nice chunk of blue. "Sure. How do I do it?"

"Go and talk to the Anglican vicar down the road, Mark Walker. He's organising a 'Churches Together' team. You really ought to join."

"I'll do that," he said, returning to the paperwork on his desk.

"No, Father, you've got to do it now because the race is next Saturday, and you should start training."

"Ah! I don't need training. I used to run to school and back every day when I was a kid," Father scoffed, but he set off to the vicarage at once.

On the morning of the race, Father was excited. He had immediately clicked with Mark and was looking forward to meeting the other members of their team and help raise funds for the interfaith children's camp.

"How are your shoulders feeling?" Belinda asked him on his way out to the pre-race meeting.

"Shoulders? Never felt better," he replied, slightly puzzled. She surely meant legs.

"Great. Best of luck!"

When he reached the big tent at the bottom of the hill, Father's puzzlement fizzled out like water on a hot pan. Cheese was not the prize—it was the load.

Those enormous cheese wheels at the start line had to be hauled up the escarpment to the scarp-edge on which the village was built.

"Emmanuel, you can run the last section

and have the pleasure of crossing the finish line," Mark told him.

Father swallowed. Those cheese wheels looked many times heavier than the backpack he used to carry to school as a child. The heaviest object he had lifted recently was the Sunday Missal. Belinda was right: he should have trained.

The whistle blew and Mark sprinted off with the cheese on his shoulders as if it was a feather pillow. At the first relay point, he effortlessly rolled it onto the shoulders of another team member, who gained terrain over the pub's team. By the third relay point, they'd overtaken the car garage's team and in the fourth section they left behind the farmers' team.

It was now Father's turn to accept the cheese for the last section of the race, the steepest and the one where the most glory— or infamy—hung. Only the sports centre's team were ahead now. Would he lose his team all the advantage they had gained? His palms broke into a sweat. The cheese wheel looked as slippery as wax. He was sure to drop it.

As the panting Quaker clerk passed him the load, for the first time Father Okoli felt its weight: it was as heavy as a small person. Slowly putting one foot in front of the other, he thought of Jesus carrying the cross and wished Simon of Cyrene was here to help. He was going to lose his team the chance to gain first place and was likely to let slip their second place, too. He focused his gaze on the finish line up at the top.

He could just about see the presbytery's back garden and his hens flapping about, as if cheering him. Then a flash of coppery fur—a fox! The yell forming in his lungs turned into an Incredible Hulk grunt, and the urge to protect his flock gave him super strength. He zoomed up the hill, overtook the sport centre's team and crossed the finish line in first place.

A massive cheer burst from the crowd and scared the fox off into the nearby copse. Father collapsed on the grass with a big smile.

There were cheers and congratulations, and the pub landlord offered the winners a complimentary lunch.

It was delicious, but Father Okoli opted for the beef rather than the chicken roast. He also passed on the cheese platter.

3. FOOD PARCELS

Belinda Clarke was firmly convinced that her duties as parish administrator went beyond her official job description. For one, looking after their new parish priest and making sure he was fed, healthy and happy, had undoubtedly fallen within her responsibilities.

That morning, the postman delivered to the parish office a large parcel addressed to Father. The stamps showed that it was from Nigeria, Father's home country. What was inside it? The custom declaration was so badly scrawled that it was illegible.

"There's a parcel for you!" she announced excitedly as soon as Father walked into the parish office.

He looked at it and tutted. "My dear old mum must be convinced that I'm starving here," he joked.

But Belinda didn't laugh. If his mother

thought that he wasn't being properly fed, going so far as sending him food parcels, it was no laughing matter.

She resolved that she would pop round to the presbytery with a hot casserole later, and tomorrow she would have Father over for dinner.

That evening, when she turned up with her casserole, Father wasn't at home. It was suppertime. Had someone invited him for dinner? The generous part of her was pleased that Father was being looked after, but the selfish part was annoyed that the person looking after him wasn't her. She strode home and put the casserole in the freezer. Better luck tomorrow.

The next morning, the postman delivered another parcel from Nigeria. Maybe she was right in thinking that Father was hungry: perhaps he didn't like British food.

"This is from my sister," Father said apologetically when Belinda handed him the parcel.

Was his entire family feeding him? She still hadn't managed to give him her casserole or to invite him to dinner. Belinda couldn't take it. Around midmorning, she excused herself and scuttled to the bakery round the corner.

"Your tea break, Father," she announced,

returning with scones, cream and jam. If she couldn't feed him at any other time, she would feed him at work.

He smiled weakly. Oh no, maybe it was true that he didn't like British food.

"If you don't like them, I'll get something else," she offered anxiously.

"No, I love scones, thank you," he said, accepting the plate she had prepared for him.

Belinda watched him carefully. At midday, he still hadn't eaten a crumb.

When she got home after work, she searched online for Nigerian recipes and rang him. "Father, we'd love to have you for dinner tonight."

"Sorry, I have a previous engagement," he replied awkwardly.

Someone had beaten her to it again! Now she was getting a little desperate.

The next day, she turned up to work with a freshly baked Nigerian coconut cake. "For your morning break, Father!" she said excitedly.

Father's eyebrows shot up and he shifted uncomfortably in his seat. "Thank you, but...I can't."

"Father, why do you let everyone else feed you but not me? Your family sends you food parcels, other people invite you for dinner, but I still haven't been able to give you anything!"

Father smiled. "Belinda, I would love to eat some of your cake, but I'm on a diet. I have been out the last two nights because it was my birthday and my other parishes insisted on throwing parties for me. I couldn't say no when they feel sad about me moving away to live here. The parcels from Nigeria aren't food. They are birthday presents. Perhaps my mum thinks I'm becoming too thin, but she knows very well that it's because I'm on a diet."

Belinda laughed. She had tied herself in knots over nothing. "Now that I know that it's your birthday, you can't deny me the pleasure of celebrating it, too. Will you come for dinner tomorrow? I'll make a slimming salad."

"I'd love to," he said with a smile.

"Wonderful. See you tomorrow at my place, then?"

"You can count on it!"

Later, for her tea break, Belinda cut herself a slice of her coconut cake and it tasted great.

4. THE BARBER OF SEVILLE

Father Okoli looked at his reflection in the mirror. He had just turned forty and was still getting used to it. Among the other clergy in his Cotswolds diocese, he was considered a whippersnapper, but back home forty years counted as a very respectable age. His own father had been a grandfather at forty.

He checked himself in the mirror. A few curls had turned white on his temples and he could do with a haircut, especially as he was going to dinner at Belinda's house that evening.

The barber welcomed him warmly. "Hello, Father. I'm Carlos, the Spanish barber of the village!" he declared.

"A pleasure to meet you." Father was used to being greeted by people he didn't know.

Carlos twirled on the heels of his leather boots and picked up a glossy photobook.

"What would you like?"

"Nothing special. I'd just like my hair a little shorter than it is now."

"A haircut to celebrate your birthday, right?"

"How do you know?"

"The village barber knows everything about everyone, just like the village priest. Only, when people come to your confessional, they tell you their own sins, while when they sit on my chair they mostly tell me other people's."

Father chuckled. "Yes, I suppose you're right."

"Take a seat," Carlos said, turning the barber's chair round for him.

Father wasn't entirely sure he wanted to sit on it anymore.

With a similar gesture to a bullfighter, Carlos whipped a red cloth off a shelf and wrapped it round Father's neck. A shiver ran down Father's back as his gaze fell on a tray in front of him, containing a cut-throat razor. I hope I'm not the bull, he thought to himself.

Carlos started snipping at his hair. "Father, do you find that the people who come for confession the most are the ones who need it the least?"

"Probably, yes."

"It's the same here. The people who need a

haircut the most come the least often. Do you know why?"

"I guess that some people need more reassurance than others that they are doing okay," Father replied.

Carlos shook his head and his quiff quivered. "No, Father. The haircut and the confession are only excuses. People come to us because they want to talk, and we listen to them. But who will listen to us? Who do you talk to, Father?"

"God."

"I mean, among our fellow humans."

"Are you married, Carlos?"

"No. Where would I meet a woman? All my clients are men, and all the women in the village are either married, or too young. It's hopeless."

Father smiled. "Don't give up. Keep your ears open, because God has His subtle ways."

Carlos glanced at the clock on the wall. "I hope you didn't want a shave too, Father, because I'm short of time."

"No, thank you," Father replied, eyeing the cut-throat razor again.

"My next customer is new to the village and I don't want to keep him waiting on his first appointment," Carlos explained.

Just then, the door jingled and a woman

and a boy stepped inside. Carlos had finished Father's haircut just in time.

"You must be Angus," Carlos said to the little boy.

"Yes. I'm named after the singer of a band that my dad liked very much."

"I know, Angus Young from AC/DC. I love them, too." Carlos smiled. "Maybe your dad and I should meet some time." Carlos turned the chair towards the boy and Angus hopped on.

"You can't, because he's in heaven."

"Oh, I'm sorry."

"It's okay. He's happy there," the boy replied.

Father's throat constricted with emotion, and he glanced at the boy's mother. She still hadn't said a word but was smiling sweetly at her boy. Suddenly, Father had a feeling that something marvellous was about to unfold in Carlos's life and that God's hand was at work right there, before his eyes. Father gazed for a moment at the barber and smiled.

"See you next time, Carlos," he said as he left, making a mental note to come back for a haircut soon.

5. A BIRTHDAY SURPRISE

Much to Nathan's relief, his mum was starting to relax. She had originally invited their new parish priest for dinner, but then decided to make it a surprise birthday party and invite the whole parish.

She had been so stressed that there had been times that day when Nathan had switched off his hearing aids to get a little peace. But now that Father's party was going well and everyone seemed to be enjoying themselves, Nathan could relax, too.

He was tucking into a chicken skewer when his mum walked over.

"Nathan, could you pop round the presbytery and lock up Father's hens for the night? He forgot."

"Okay."

He wiped his mouth carefully as he thought it indelicate to turn up at Father's chicken coop with traces of his chicken dinner on his lips, and set off briskly.

When he got to the presbytery, the hens were already roosting in their coop. All he had to do was bolt the door. Easy-peasy.

He had turned to leave when a proud "cluck" resounded in the evening air. It didn't come from the coop.

Nathan scanned the place. A white hen looked down on him defiantly from the roof of the kitchen extension. Nathan tried to coax her. "Come down, little hen."

"Cluck!" the hen replied, taking a step back.

Nathan clambered onto the water butt and pulled himself up onto the roof. The hen backed away. He should have brought some grains. Too late now. He clicked his tongue and offered a hand, pretending he had food. The hen cocked her head and hopped to the main roof.

"You're playing hard to get, but I'll win."

He stepped onto the roof, thankful for his lithe frame. But the hen continued to hop away until she had reached the other side of the roof, which backed onto the main road. A tractor was trundling down, pulling a trailer of hay bales.

"Come on," Nathan coaxed the hen. She had nowhere left to go. She had to come down to him.

But the hen didn't. She let out a squawk and, in a flurry of wings, landed on the passing hay bales.

"Come back!" Nathan shouted, scrambling down from the roof. He ran after the tractor, waving his arms, but Farmer Price didn't notice until they got to the farm.

"What's the matter, young man?"

"I need that hen back." Nathan panted.

"We'll never get her out of there tonight. Come back tomorrow morning."

What if Father counted his hens when he got home tonight? That would be the worst birthday surprise. "Do you have hens?" Nathan asked the farmer.

"Yes."

"Can we do a swap? You keep this one and I'll take one of yours, just for the night. In the morning, I'll swap them back."

Farmer Price seemed a little confused but agreed. Nathan chose a similar-looking hen and took her back to the presbytery, where he locked her safely in the coop for the night.

The next day, Nathan waited until nine o'clock—just to be sure that Father was out—before sneaking into the presbytery's back garden to swap the hens.

But Father was there.

"Good morning, Nathan. You won't guess what happened: I've got a new hen!" He picked up Farmer Price's hen and stroked her. "I've called her Thérèse, after St. Thérèse of Lisieux, the patron saint of missions, because she must have had a missionary spirit to go adventuring into my garden."

Oh no. How was he going to return the hen to Farmer Price now that Father had taken her into his flock and even…baptised her? Nathan smiled weakly.

"There's more: this morning I found Clare outside the coop, pecking at the door to be let in. Last night, you must have counted Thérèse in her place and locked her out. Thank goodness the fox didn't get her!" Father said with a smile.

Nathan shot Clare a reproachful glance, but the hen just clucked. Now Farmer Price was short of one hen! Nathan would have to explain and offer to pay for Thérèse.

"Father named my hen?" Farmer Price laughed heartily when Nathan told him what had happened. "No worries, I don't want any money. It'll be a birthday present for Father that only we know about."

6. A VILLAGE AFFAIR

"Parish of the Ascension, how may I help?" Belinda answered.

"Hello, I have a funeral request, but it's a little special. I'm the sister of Father O'Connor." The woman hesitated. "You were his last parish before he retired back in Ireland, fifteen years ago."

"I see. I only moved to this parish ten years ago," Belinda explained. She remembered hearing about a much-loved priest who had been there before her days. It must be him.

"My brother has just passed away and he expressed the wish to have his funeral in your parish. I had hoped the new priest wouldn't mind…"

"Not at all." Father Okoli hadn't struck her as someone who would be jealous of his congregation's affection towards a predecessor. Belinda expressed her condolences and they set a date for the funeral.

As she had anticipated, Father was more than happy about it. "It will be nice for the parish to remember Father O'Connor together."

The news spread like wildfire. Those who had known Father O'Connor were sad at his passing but touched that he had chosen their parish for his funeral.

By lunchtime, the news had spread to the entire village. Reverend Mark called to give his condolences, sympathy cards piled through the letter-box and even the atheist pub landlord asked for the funeral details. By the evening, it was clear that the funeral would be not just a parish event, but a whole village one.

Belinda rang Father Okoli. "I'm worried there won't be enough space in church. Do you think we can spill out into the garden?"

"Of course. I celebrated plenty of outdoor Masses back in Nigeria."

"The weather might not be quite the same…" Belinda said.

"It'll be fine. Have we got enough chairs?"

"Perhaps not. I'll find out if we can hire them."

"Excellent, Belinda. It'll all be fine," Father declared jauntily.

Belinda wondered if Father's optimism was less to do with reasoning and more to do with trust in God's Providence.

But the next day, it became clear that things were not going to be fine. When Father O'Connor's other previous parishes heard the news, the attendee headcount shot through the roof. Even with all hands on deck, they were going to be stretched. The last straw was the weather forecast: a heavy downpour was due on the morning of the funeral.

"Can we hire an all-weather marquee?" Father asked Belinda, looking a little less cheerful this time.

"I'll try." Belinda was doubtful that they'd find anything available at such short notice.

While she was plodding home for lunch, pondering these questions with a heavy heart, a voice called her.

"Hello Belinda, are you all right?" It was Reverend Mark.

Belinda poured her heart out to him.

"If Father won't feel like we're stealing the limelight, we'd be happy to open our church for you."

Belinda's heart leaped. "Oh, Father will be delighted! Thank you!"

The Anglican church had been built back when their village was the major cheese market for the region. As a result, the church was enormous.

Belinda forgot all about her lunch and skipped back to the parish office feeling light as a bird.

When the news spread that Father Okoli had accepted Reverend Mark's help, the Methodists and the Quakers felt brave enough to offer their help, too. The Methodists opened their car park, while the Quakers set up their hall for the coffees and teas. Now the funeral had a big enough church to accommodate everyone in the dry and enough stewards to make everything run smoothly.

Relieved of all those tasks, Belinda, Father and the other parish members could concentrate on the music and the liturgy, and on remembering their beloved parish priest.

7. DRIVING LESSONS

"You look down—is everything all right?" Father asked Nathan as he was getting ready to serve at the Sunday Mass.

"I want to learn to drive, but the insurance on Dad's car for a learner driver is too expensive. I want to be able to drive to the cinema with my friends." Nathan had one particular friend in mind, Katie Jenkins, but he wasn't going to say that.

Father scratched his chin. "I'll see if there's anything I can do."

After Mass, Nathan saw Father talk to his parents, and when he returned, he had a big grin. "I'll teach you to drive in my car. I'll pick you up at three o'clock."

Father would teach him to drive? He couldn't have heard correctly. He turned up the volume of his hearing aids and asked Father to repeat what he'd said. Yes, he had heard right!

So at three o'clock Father turned up in his red Mini. "Hop in. You'll have your turn when we get there," Father said.

"Where?" Nathan asked, jumping into the car.

"I can't teach you on public roads without insurance, so I've asked Farmer Jenkins if we can use his land."

Nathan's breath caught in his chest. Farmer Jenkins was Katie's dad. The last thing Nathan wanted was for the farmer, let alone Katie, to see him stalling the car and making a fool of himself. "Er…I don't think it's a good idea to inconvenience Farmer Jenkins."

Father gave him a clap on the shoulder. "Don't you worry, young man. There's nothing that you can damage in the fields."

When they got there, Nathan saw that Father was right: on those muddy dirt tracks, the only thing that could be damaged was his own pride.

"Just like the roads where I learned to drive!" Father exclaimed.

They swapped seats and Nathan practised with the clutch and the gears. It was hard to keep the car travelling straight on the mud, but fear turned into exhilaration and excitement, and Nathan felt like a rally driver.

Suddenly, a tractor peeked over the crest of

the field. Farmer Jenkins!

Nathan's hands turned clammy and he pinned his gaze on the track, determined not to skid in front of Katie's father.

"She's waving at us," Father told him, waving at the tractor.

"She?"

"Farmer Jenkins' daughter."

The car lurched, jolted and came to a stop, as Nathan instantly forgot everything he had learned. All he could think was that Katie was watching.

"Hello," Katie said with a smile, stopping on the other side of the hawthorn hedge. She turned off her engine, probably so that Nathan could hear her. "Dad would like to speak to Nathan when you've finished. I can drop him off home on the tractor later, if that's okay?" she said.

"Sure!" Nathan answered. "You don't mind, Father, do you?"

"Not at all. This is a good time to end your driving lesson, isn't it?" Father Okoli said with a wink.

Nathan felt his cheeks warm up. "Yes, please."

In the blink of an eye, he was out of the car and next to Katie in the tractor cab.

Farmer Jenkins was waiting for them at the

top of the hill. "Hello, young man. I saw you drive Father's car. It wasn't at all bad for a first time. Would you like to earn some money this summer and help us with the harvest?"

"Sure!" Nathan replied without any hesitation.

Whether it was picking strawberries or mucking out stables, he'd do anything to be around Katie.

"Great," Farmer Jenkins continued. "I reckon that, with practice, you'll be able to drive the tractor next to the combine harvester."

Nathan's jaw dropped. "Drive the tractor?"

"It's easier than it looks. I'll teach you," Katie said, and Nathan's heart somersaulted in his chest.

As a young boy, he had dreamed of driving a tractor. Recently, he had dreamed of spending time with Katie. This summer, he was going to do both!

8. SOMETHING FOR THE YOUTH

"Thank you for giving Nathan a head-start with driving. We've now booked him for driving lessons and a driving test. He's planning to buy a second-hand car with the money he'll earn this summer at the Jenkins farm," Belinda told Father. "The young people here are desperate to drive off to the city. The village has little to offer them."

Father thought about it. "Do you think we could do more for the young people of our parish?"

"Perhaps, yes."

Father picked up his diary and opened it. "Okay, let's put the situation right. I want a parish council meeting to discuss it."

It was heartening to see so many people turn up to the meeting. After beginning the meeting with a prayer, the chair of the parish council opened the discussion to the floor with a question. "What could we organise for our young people?"

Father thought back to his own youth. Every afternoon he had played football with his friends in the fields of the mission school. Sometimes the priests joined them, too. "How about football?"

Some of the men nodded, but none of the women did.

"How about an afternoon tea at my café? I'll throw in tea and scones for free," Janet, the owner of the tea shop, offered.

"You don't have to do that, Janet. We can do a soup lunch in the church hall. The Union of Catholic Mothers can provide homemade soup," Gracie suggested.

"I think kids would rather have pizza," Belinda said.

Father was still convinced that a football match would be more fun, but a pizza evening sounded easy to organise and the Union had volunteered to order the pizzas and tidy up afterwards, so it was decided.

The next Sunday evening, all the teens of the parish duly turned up, but they looked as enthusiastic as if they were going to school. The rest of the evening didn't go much better. Trays of delicious pizza lay untouched. One or two kids tucked in, but the majority just nibbled nervously at a single slice. Conversation was as scarce as appetite and everybody sat in silence in a circle, looking at their plates. What was wrong?

At the end of the pitiful evening, Father decided to tap on teenagers' legendary honesty.

"Guys and girls, can I ask a question that requires an honest answer?"

They nodded.

"Have you enjoyed tonight?"

Nathan looked up. "Not really," he mumbled. "Sitting in a circle feels like school."

"That's good to know: we'll take it into account for next time. Anything else?"

"Eating in front of other people is embarrassing," said a girl with braces.

"Especially with all the adults watching us."

All the other kids nodded in agreement and Father was heartened to see them so responsive and willing to share their opinions.

"I am really thankful for your honesty," he said.

"Thank you for organising it. You meant well," the girl with braces said.

"What are you going to do with the leftover food?" one of the boys asked.

"Take as much as you want and I'll drop

the rest off to a homeless shelter in the city. I'm due to volunteer there tonight," one of the ladies of the UCM said.

The girl with braces sat up. "Can I come too? I'd love to help out there!"

"Me, too!"

"And me!"

Father exchanged glances with the UCM lady and they nodded to each other. "Yes, it's a great idea. But we'll need to check with your parents."

They drove down to the city in four cars, chatting happily. At the shelter, they were put to work buttering bread and serving soup. The guests were keener to chat with the kids than they were with their usual volunteers. Some of them were the same age.

On the way back, they resolved that they would go again, perhaps regularly. As he was driving home with his car full of starry-eyed teenagers who felt that they had perhaps started changing the world, Father reflected. Instead of organising something for the youth, they should have organised something with them.

9. THE PARISH BARBEQUE

Belinda mixed another jug of orange squash and put it down on the drinks table. Everything was ready for the parish barbecue.

Father had been on edge all week, checking the weather forecast, fretting about the number of chairs and tables, repeatedly asking for the list of food.

On his very first day in the parish he had told her of his wish to give a party for his three parishes, but he'd waited for the Spring Bank Holiday to ensure the highest possible turnout.

Now the day had arrived, and a healthy queue was forming outside the gate. Father must be pleased.

"It's twelve o'clock," Erika called from the gate.

"Great. We can start," Belinda replied, taking position at the drinks stall.

People of all ages flocked in, some she

recognised, but many she had never seen before. 'Please, God, let it go well for Father's sake. He's a good man,' she thought.

The tables filled up, children ran around, and an eager queue snaked to the hot dog stall. Happy sounds of chattering and laughter filled the warm spring air. The party was going well. Father must be happy—wherever he was.

"Any idea where Father is?" she asked Erika, who was serving the wine.

"Nope."

Belinda scanned the place. It seemed everyone was having a jolly time but in their own groups. The three parishes weren't getting to know each other at all!

After lunch, they should start a team-building game. She must tell Father.

Belinda left the drinks stall in Erika's hands and went looking for Father. Walking past a table, she heard someone grumble. "No wonder Father prefers his new parish! Look at the beautiful church, the presbytery and this big garden!"

"We're like the old wife and this is like the pretty young new one. We just can't compete!" a woman said.

Belinda stopped in her tracks. Poor Father. Like a child at the arrival of a new baby sibling, his other parishes were feeling jealous and neglected. This must be why he had wanted the barbecue—to make all his children feel included, cherished and wanted. But if anything, the rift might be growing! They had to do something about it before everyone went home. But where was Father?

She asked around but nobody had seen him. When she didn't find him in the church or the presbytery either, she panicked. She ran back to the garden.

"Has anyone seen Father?" she shouted.

Silence fell instantly, and people shook their heads.

"I can't find him anywhere. He would never miss this barbecue."

Heads nodded.

"Let's go looking for him!" someone said from one of the other parishes.

They got up and left everything behind. Food half-eaten, drinks half-drunk, handbags on chairs, walking sticks and footballs abandoned. People from the three parishes joined each other to search for the man they cared so much about.

Their calls echoed in the belfry, in the gents' toilets, in the chicken coop, until a cry of "I've found Father!" came from one of the kids.

There was Father, sitting in his car, fast asleep.

"Poor Father, he works so hard for us all!" said the same person Belinda had caught grumbling earlier.

"Oh, bless him! He must have been parking the car after driving me here. I didn't have a lift, so he picked me up," an elderly gentleman said.

"I'll give you a lift next time," a young man offered.

Everyone was relieved to have found Father safe and sound. They decided to let him sleep a little longer, then send one of the kids to wake him up, so that he wouldn't be embarrassed. It would be the three parishes' little secret.

When they returned to their tables, Belinda noticed that the elderly gentleman was sitting with the young man, and the groups were all mingling. It seemed that searching together for the man they all loved had been the best possible team-building exercise.

10. THE BEST DRESSED WINDOW

It was the time of year for the "Best Dressed Window" competition again. Anne looked at her shop window and sighed. Livers, kidneys and chicken breasts didn't make an attractive show. Maybe if she stretched a string of sausages around the edges like fairy lights? She could add a touch of colour with a spray of parsley here and there, and a scattering of lemon slices…

She shook her head. No, a few sprigs of parsley wasn't going to cut it. The competition was fierce. Last year the rosette had gone to the post office. In their window, they had set up an egg incubator, full of fertilised chicken eggs, inside a parcel box to show how carefully they handled fragile deliveries. Passers-by could watch the eggs hatch into the cutest little yellow chicks. So many children and parents had stopped on their way to and from school, that traffic wardens had been called to direct the traffic around them. How could she compete with that?

"What's the matter, dear?" her husband asked her.

It was time to close the shop and she was staring hopelessly at their window. "I don't know what to do about the competition. The organisers are going round the village to take pictures tomorrow."

"We don't have to take part," he said, trying to be helpful.

"But I'd like to. Have you got any ideas?" she said.

He rubbed his hands on his apron. "Sorry. If I was a man of ideas, I would be working in an office."

After thirty-five years of marriage, Anne knew that wasn't true. Rob loved the shop he had inherited and he was full of good ideas.

"You could touch up the opening hours on the door, perhaps," he suggested.

Yes, that was a good start. She turned the shop sign to Closed and got to work with her paintbrushes. Thankfully, she had a steady hand and even the curves of the zeros were impeccably neat.

She had just finished when an idea flashed across her mind. She could paint on her shop window all the things that she couldn't put there for real! She told Rob to go home and have dinner without her, then she dug out all the other paint colours. With a pang of sadness, she thought of her husband eating his dinner alone. He'd loved it when their daughters were still at home and they ate together every night.

That was it! She would paint a family sitting together for their dinner, with a succulent lamb roast taking pride of place in the middle of the table. She rescued a small table from the back of the shop and pushed it up to the window, dressed it with a cheerful gingham tablecloth, laid out cutlery and crockery then painted the family gathered around it, starting with the children, who looked just like her own girls.

The next day, she was at the shop at the crack of dawn to finish her painting before the photographers did their rounds. When Rob arrived to open the shop, she was about to paint the parents.

"You've done a great job," he said.

"I'm afraid I won't make it in time," she fretted.

He stepped up into the window, his arm around her waist, and kissed her. "You will."

But around midday, when she was still painting the father, a customer walked in.

"What a shame the photographers have already been," he said. "Your window is coming on very nicely."

"Oh, no! I didn't make it!" Anne whimpered.

Rob rushed to hug her. "You can try again next year. I love your window and I'm sure that it'll attract more customers."

That evening, Anne was still too sad to speak to anyone when the phone rang, so Rob answered. He returned to the room with a beaming smile. "We've won first prize in the People's Choice category!"

They checked the competition's website and there was a photo of their window! It had been taken before Anne had painted the parents. There she stood with Rob, looking like they belonged to the little scene of family love, caught right at the moment of their kiss.

The caption read: *The People's Choice award goes to butchers Anne and Rob Stokes, for their "Happy Family Mealtime" living window.*

11. DRESSED TO IMPRESS

"It's your First Holy Communion. Are you excited?" Father asked the children after their catechism class.

"Yes! I'm going to wear a dress made of lace!" one of the girls announced.

"My dress touches the floor, like a princess!" another one said.

"Then you need shoes with heels. Mine are all sparkly, with pearls and sequins," another girl said.

"I've got pearls, too, and white gloves," another said.

The other girls and boys joined in the sartorial one-upmanship before Father's bewildered eyes. "Clothes are not what matters," he said at last.

"That's what my mum says, but that's because she hasn't got enough money to buy me the dress I want," one girl said.

Father shook his head. "You children

shouldn't forget what First Holy Communion is really about."

"It's about receiving Jesus," one child said. "But we must show respect by wearing expensive clothes."

Father sighed. He had to talk to Belinda about this. He dismissed the class and went to the parish office.

Belinda nodded when he explained the issue to her. "I know of people who put off their children receiving the sacrament because they can't afford the expense of the clothes and the party. There are a lot of expectations from family and friends…"

"We can throw a party for them: tea and cakes in the church hall!" Father suggested excitedly.

"I fear that might not be enough. For some people, a First Holy Communion party has to be almost as lavish as a wedding reception."

No, he couldn't allow families to bear that burden. If, each year, there was a party in the church hall that ticked all the boxes and got families off the hook, people wouldn't have to worry about money. The parish would worry about the practical matters, like Martha in the Gospel, and parents and children could enjoy what was actually important, like Martha's sister, Mary.

He immediately rang Douglas, the chair of the parish council.

"I can't say that we will be able to do it every year," Douglas said, "but this time we've got spare cash after cancelling the pilgrimage."

"Thank you!"

Father was straight on the phone to a childhood friend who was now a well-known DJ in Bristol. He immediately agreed to provide music and lighting.

Belinda was happy to organise the food, the St Vincent De Paul Society volunteered to serve at the tables, and the Union of Catholic Mothers put their names down for the washing-up.

When Father rang the parents and told them about the party, some thanked him but preferred to carry on with their previous arrangement, while the rest sounded relieved and grateful.

Now there was only one problem left. The clothes for the children. Father turned to Belinda again. "Didn't you once tell me that, in past years, there have been as many as fifteen altar servers on the altar at once? Does this mean we still have the fifteen albs they wore?"

"Yes. All in need of a wash and a few

stitches."

"Do you reckon that the Union of Catholic Mothers could give them some love and care?"

Belinda smiled. "I'm sure they'd love to."

When Father informed the parents that no child was allowed to wear their own clothes during the ceremony, but the parish would provide suitable attire, some grumbled, some were quick to return their expensive clothes to the shops and others breathed a sigh of relief.

On the day of the first Holy Communion, the children processed into the church wearing the carefully restored albs.

After the ceremony, the albs were promptly collected before food or drink could be spilled on them, and were safely put away for next year's batch. Then everyone was off to the church hall for the party. The hall was beautifully decorated with flowers and bunting, the food was delicious and the music was great. A successful outcome for all, thought Father happily.

12. THE MUSIC BUG

Father Okoli walked into the parish office, where Belinda was on the phone.

"Yes, the window on the top of the church is stuck. We need someone to come and see to it before the rain arrives," she said.

Yesterday had been a hot day, and the church was so full for the children's First Holy Communion that they had had to open the windows in the roof to let air circulate. Now one was stuck open.

Apart from that, the day had been a great success, including the party in the church hall afterwards. Everyone had had fun, and Father had enjoyed welcoming to the stage his childhood friend, now a well-respected DJ and musician. Near the end, his friend had asked him to join him in singing an old Nigerian folk song. Father obliged and enjoyed it very much. It had been years since he had last sung anything in his native language.

"Hello, Father. I wasn't expecting you today. How are you?" Belinda said, her phone call finished.

"Well, thank you. Why weren't you expecting me?"

"My son told me that you've got a virus."

"What virus?"

"I don't know. He said you'd gone viral."

They looked at each other, then Belinda slapped her forehead and chuckled. "Now I think about it, he must have meant something about the internet."

Just then, Father's mobile phone rang. It was his DJ friend. "Hey, we've gone viral!"

Father remembered that someone at the party had asked him for permission to post a video of him. Thinking nothing of it, he had said yes. The clip had been seen by thousands of people and even been reposted by his friend's record label's team.

"My manager wants you to sing for us. Just a few vocals here and there. I told him that you're a busy priest and probably need permission from the Pope, or something. But hey, I had to tell you."

Making music with his friend? That was a wacky idea, but enticing!

No, there was no way he could justify

spending time on that. With the three parishes he was already up to his eyes with work, and he still dreamed of starting a PhD in Canon Law.

"Thanks for the offer. I'm very honoured, but—"

"Father, wait," Belinda whispered. "Have a think. Don't answer quite yet."

Father told his friend that he would think about it, then ended the call and turned to Belinda.

"Music is a great way to spread the gospel. Your voice is a gift from God, so you must use it. You could touch so many hearts."

Put that way, having musical fun with his friend didn't feel like a whim. Even the bishop sounded positive about the idea. The only thing stopping Father from joining the limelight was a touch of shyness. But that wasn't a virtue of saints and missionaries, so he mustered courage and called his friend. "I have decided to take up your offer, but with a condition: I'll write the lyrics."

"Deal done, bro!"

"What? Aren't you even asking me what I'm planning to write?" Father had expected to face more resistance.

"No. I know you're going to write religious songs. I don't mind. But we have to act quickly; the internet is fickle. You're viral today and you're nobody tomorrow."

Father wrote the lyrics of his first song on the train to Bristol, and that very afternoon he and his friend were recording. By the end of the week, they had an entire album. Father had had a blast and was very pleased with the album, but exhausted.

By the Sunday Mass, the church window was still stuck because he hadn't had time to approve the window repair quote. Luckily, there was no sign of rain and the weather was still so hot that Father was drooping under his vestments. Tired, sweaty and hoarse from a week of recording, he looked a state when he started to sing the entrance hymn in a croaky voice. Worried murmurs spread in the congregation.

"Is Father all right?" Belinda's husband asked.

She smiled.

"First he went viral, and now he's got the music bug."

13. THE SCARECROW COMPETITION

Belinda It was that time of year again when Moreton-on-the-Edge became inhabited by scarecrows. They adorned every front garden, except Belinda Clarke's.

The village scarecrow trail was a fun activity for the villagers and for tourists, but it was also a competition. And Belinda hated competitions, especially when contestants took them seriously, like her neighbours.

Grant next door, for example, started working on his scarecrows as soon as he had put away the Christmas lights. He didn't just make one or two, but entire scenes inspired by films or novels. Belinda couldn't match it.

"Why don't we make some scarecrows this year, Mum?" her son, Nathan, sprang on her, just a week before the entry deadline. Belinda was convinced that Nathan's sudden interest in scarecrows was to do with Farmer Jenkins, Katie's dad, being the supplier of straw for the village. Chances were her son would forget about the scarecrows as soon as he'd bought the straw, and she could let the matter drop.

But she was wrong. Nathan came back from the farm empty-handed. The winter barley crop had been poor, and the little straw there had been was all sold to early birds like Grant.

"We need to find something else to fill our scarecrows with," Nathan said.

As Belinda and Nathan asked around the village for advice, they discovered that the vicar, the butcher and the pub landlord and landlady had also been left straw-less.

"We're filling ours with wool. They can sit under the shop's awning, so they'll stay dry," the butcher said.

"We've got some tatty old cushions that could do with replacing. We'll use the filling," the pub landlady told them.

But Belinda and Nathan didn't have cushion filling, wool or an awning.

"I've got some rockwool in the loft," Belinda's husband, Declan, said.

So, while father and son built the frame and stuffed Mr and Mrs Scarecrow, Belinda stitched mouths and eyes on jute sacks. With old clothes, the Clarkes had two perfectly normal, totally average, T-shaped scarecrows.

On the flip side, this year the rest of their street had gone above and beyond. Grant's "Pride and Prejudice" picnic scene looked ordinary next to the Barringtons' Indiana Jones eight-character scene.

"We are the shame of the street," Belinda murmured.

"I'm sure everyone is happy we're not going to steal the first prize," Declan said.

The morning of the judging, cries of "vandals!" rose from the village.

Scarecrows were missing limbs, clothes and heads. The village was in uproar. Months of work had been destroyed overnight and, crucially, before the judging had taken place. It turned out that the "vandals" were some goats escaped from Farmer Jenkins' farm. It seemed they were taking back the straw that their farmer had perhaps too generously given away.

The goats were safely taken back to their farm and the judging was put off to the following day, to give the contestants a chance to repair their displays.

Of course, Farmer Jenkins couldn't provide any extra straw, so the worst scarecrow casualties were sacrificed and used to repair their companions.

The Clarke's scarecrows hadn't been

touched: goats clearly didn't like rockwool.

"I desperately need a new Liz Bennet. Would you mind lending me your lady scarecrow?" Grant asked Belinda and her husband.

The Barringtons, too, turned to the Clarkes for help: they desperately needed a new Indiana Jones. The Clarkes' Mrs Scarecrow got to wear a beautiful Regency frock, and Mr Scarecrow was promoted to Indiana Jones, both taking pride of place in the best displays of the village.

Competition turned into team work, and Belinda and her family got a share in both first and second prize.

14. THE SWIMMING LESSON

Not far from Moreton-on-the-Edge, some old quarries had been turned into lakes for recreational use. On a hot summer like they were having, Father thought it would be nice for the youth of the parish to go kayaking. He had never done water sports but the lake centres had trained staff.

Everyone was excited.

"Is this trip just for our parish or can we invite a friend?" Nathan asked him.

Father knew which friend Nathan had in mind. "If there's space in the minibus, you can invite her," he said.

Nathan gave him a hopeful puppy-eyed look.

"And if there's no space, we'll make it," Father added.

"Thank you!"

When the trip came round, Father had rented a bigger minibus and all the teens in the village piled in.

"Sorry but all the single kayaks are taken. You'll have to use the doubles," the centre's staff told them when they got there. Nathan and Katie took a step closer to each other.

"We're an odd number," Jake pointed out.

"You'll have to go in the water, too. The double kayaks are difficult to steer for one person on their own," the staff told Father.

"But I've never kayaked before," he said. This was the least of his problems: he couldn't swim!

"I'll show everyone what to do. We can give you wetsuits, and lifejackets!"

Lifejackets. Images from the movie "Titanic" flitted across his brain. "Have any of your kayaks ever sunk?" he asked.

The guy chuckled. "They're made of plastic filled with air. Unsinkable!"

That was exactly what the engineers had said about the Titanic.

"Father, if you don't come, one of us will have to stay back," Jake said.

That wouldn't do. He was the shepherd and, if his sheep took to the water and became fish, he would follow them and become a fisherman, which Jesus had also called his apostles to be. Whichever way he looked at it, it was his duty to join in.

Father borrowed a pair of swimmers, put on a life jacket and took his place on the kayak with Jake. It was scary at first, but as soon as he and Jake had found their rhythm with the oars, it became fun.

Nathan and Katie disappeared behind a beautiful curtain of weeping willow. Other kids jumped off their kayaks and frolicked in the water. Father felt sorry for Jake, stuck on a kayak with him.

Suddenly, Nathan and Zac jumped out of the water like crocodiles on an ambush and overturned Father's kayak.

The next moment, Father found himself in the green water. And panicked.

While his lifejacket rose up his chest, he felt hands pulling his legs down. The more he thrashed, the more they got hold of him. "Lord save me!" he thought, just like Peter had called out when he had started to sink after walking on the water. Just like then, the Lord's hand pulled him out.

Only, it wasn't the Lord's arm. It was Nathan's.

"Are you all right, Father?" he asked, guiding him to the kayak.

Father nodded, spluttering.

"Sorry… we just wanted to play a practical joke."

"It's okay, we're all alive," Father said, holding on to the kayak for dear life. As he looked down into the water, he saw that the "hands" that had pulled him down were the fronds of some aquatic plants that had wrapped themselves around his legs.

And there were his feet, paddling just above the tops of the plants. Was he…swimming?

Just for a moment, he let go of the kayak. The lifejacket helped, of course, but he was doing it!

"I'm swimming!" he cried.

"Couldn't you swim before?" the kids asked.

"No," Father admitted.

"Then we must come back next week, so Father can practise," Jake said.

"Yes! Yes!" cried the others, fists pumping the air.

Father smiled. "I'll think about it. But only if you promise not to play any more jokes!" But he could see that Nathan had left his hearing aid on the shore.

Oh, well, even if they played another trick, next time he'd be fine, because now, by chance or miracle, he could swim.

15. CYCLING ROCKET

When Grant decided that it was time to stop driving, he exchanged his car for a bicycle. This new chapter of his life was going to be his fittest. But living in Moreton-on-the-Edge meant that every return trip was uphill.

One day, as he was struggling up the steep hill with his groceries in the panniers, he met Belinda Clarke, who suggested he should get an electric bike. That afternoon, he was back at the bicycle shop, trading up for an e-bike.

The electric motor made it heavier, but at the switch of a button, the machine would propel him uphill without him so much as breaking a sweat.

He would have continued to use his e-bike just for shopping, if one day he hadn't met Belinda's boy, Nathan, also on his bike and punching the air.

"What's going on?" Grant asked.

"I've beaten my friends!" he beamed.

"Where are they?" Grant looked at the

empty road.

Nathan explained that there was an app that measured your cycling performance and compared it with other cyclists on the same route. Grant wanted to try it. Nobody needed to know that his bike was assisted by a motor. When he signed up for the cycling app, he chose "Cycling Rocket" as his pseudonym, and selected the over-75 category. Now he could compete with his peers.

Day after day, Grant broke records. Uphill, on the flat, downhill, he was always the fastest. Within weeks, Cycling Rocket had got to the top of the over-75 category and was also beating the champions of some of the younger categories. While in his real life nothing had changed, in the cycling app's world Grant was a celebrity.

But the two worlds were about to collide.

Companies that sold cycling gear kept an eye on the app's top performers, in search of the newest celebrity to sponsor. Grant's stellar ascent couldn't fail to catch the attention of Cycloton's marketing team.

They decided to contact him to ask him to endorse their products in exchange for freebies. But when Grant saw their message, he assumed it was junk mail and deleted it without reading it.

Cycloton's marketing team interpreted his silence as playing hard-to-get. In their second message, they offered him money. Again, Grant deleted it.

By now, Cycloton were desperate to get a piece of Cycling Rocket before their competitors, so they called an emergency meeting. It was agreed that their most charming employee would travel to Cycling Rocket's village and try to persuade him to accept their offer.

Grant heard from the pub landlord that a young lady was scouring the village looking for a certain Cycling Rocket. Cold shivers ran down his back. Had she been sent by the cycling app to verify that he hadn't cheated? He had to find her and come clean.

Luckily, it was easier for him to track her down than the other way round.

"I know who you're looking for," he told her, walking into the post office where she was making enquiries. As they walked to his home together, he told her about his electric bike. "That's how I got to the top of the charts. I've cheated. I'm sorry."

He was expecting an outraged response, or at least a reprimand. Instead, the young lady chuckled.

"I see. Well, you're a celebrity now, so

Cycloton is still interested in you. If I pretend that you never told me anything, would you be willing to train on one of our ultra-light, top-of-the-range bicycles until you can ride up this hill reasonably fast and we can take a video of you?"

So she was still willing to sponsor him. Grant was so relieved to have been let off the hook that he would have said yes to anything.

In the following weeks, Grant underwent a gruelling training regime and a draconian diet under the supervision of a personal trainer. Grant took it as the just deserts for his little fib.

Six weeks later, he was the fittest he had ever been, and the whole village was gathered to welcome him as he puffed and panted on his new bike. Cycloton took photos and videos in which the village featured too, and the pub got some publicity.

Grant had enjoyed his ultra-light, top-of-the-range bicycle so much that he decided to continue using it instead of his ebike.

When the Cycloton people had gone, he indulged in a hearty pub lunch with pudding. He'd burn off the calories later.

16. THE VILLAGE FÊTE

The weather was wonderful on the day of the fête. Visitors flocked to the village green—great news for the village's fundraising effort. If they raised enough money, the National Lottery would match it and they could renovate the old picture house. The village would have a cinema again.

It had closed before Anne Stokes, who ran the local butcher's shop with her husband, was born, more than sixty years ago. Her parents' first date had been there, so it was a cause that Anne cared about.

But she looked at the snake of children lining up in front of her face-painting stall and sighed. The queue had been long all morning, and hadn't grown any shorter.

Anne hadn't volunteered to run the face-painting stall. Since her shop had won the Best Dressed Window competition thanks to her artwork, she'd been asked by the fête committee, and hadn't felt she could refuse. Unfortunately, unlike a pane of glass, children's faces were soft, curved and always moving.

"We're almost done," she told the grocer's youngest, who was squirming on the little stool. Anne quickly swapped her brushes to paint the lion's whiskers. "Done!" She handed the boy a mirror.

"I look like a real lion!"

Anne smiled. Sending people away happy was the best part of the job. It almost made her forget that she hadn't had a break since the early morning.

Belinda appeared with a cup of tea and a biscuit. "I've been to the tea tent. You should see it!"

"I can't leave," Anne said, gesturing to the queue. She gulped down her tea. "Tell me what's happening," she urged Belinda.

"Grant hasn't won the marrow competition this year, and he's not pleased."

"Who won?"

"James and Erika Loft."

"They must be pleased."

"They would be, if James hadn't found out that Erika gave his old 'Beano' comics to the second-hand bookstall. They're worth a fortune. Father Okoli won the Prettiest Hen competition. He's the only one who's happy. Farmer Price's wife told me his hen looks very much like one her husband lost a while ago. Some people just can't lose."

Anne chuckled and one of the parents in the queue tutted.

"I'd better leave you," Belinda said.

"Right young man," Anne said to her next customer. "What would you like?"

"I don't know," the child squeaked.

Father Okoli stopped by. "Have you had a break since opening?" he asked. "Let me take over. I was a dab hand at painting when I was younger."

"Really?" she replied.

Father Okoli nodded, so Anne thanked him and rushed to the Portaloos.

The first block was out of order, and the next had a queue. By the time she made it back to her stall, the queue had halved. Had Father done such a bad job that everyone had run away?

"What happened?" she asked him gingerly.

"They've been served." He brushed a splash of red under the rocket he had painted on a child's cheek. "Your rocket is lit, young man. You can shoot off."

"Blast off!" the boy said, leaping off the chair.

"How did you do it?" Anne asked.

"I gave them only two choices: a rocket or a daisy. They are the only things I can draw."

"But you said you were a dab hand at painting when you were young."

"Yes. In primary school." He winked.

She looked at the children on the merry-go-round. Those who had their cheeks painted with Father's simple daisy or his wonky rocket were just as happy as those with intricate butterflies, lions, and panthers.

Maybe she had painted those complicated designs for her own pride and satisfaction more than for the children.

"Thanks, Father."

"No problem." He handed her back the brushes.

Feeling lighter, she called the next child forward. "Would you like a daisy or a rocket?"

17. FATHER AT THE BAR

Father Okoli thought about something Belinda had once said. "The pub landlord knows more about our husbands than we do."

With Belinda's husband, Declan, he hadn't moved beyond polite pleasantries. Maybe he should reach out to his parishioners in the places where they felt more comfortable.

James Loft, the pub landlord, greeted him. "Father! How nice to see you. What can I get you?"

"Something local," Father said, taking a stool at the bar. If you wanted to talk to people, the bar was the place.

James poured him a pint of the local scrumpy. It was cloudy, dry and very strong. Father didn't enjoy it at all.

James' wife, Erika, emerged from the kitchen and greeted him with a smile that disappeared as soon as her husband talked to her. She walked away.

James sighed. "She's still cross with me for the scene I made at the fête."

Father had heard the story. How Erika, not knowing their sentimental and collector's value, had donated her husband's "Beano" comics to the book stall at the fête, and when he had spotted them, he had made a scene, much to Erika's embarrassment.

"You two should talk," Father said.

"We haven't got time."

Just then, a large party walked through the door and James left him. Father watched husband and wife working alongside each other but keeping their distance. It was sad.

"I could hold the fort while you and Erika iron things out," Father told James when he was free.

"Really?" James beamed. "Could you come tomorrow at three?"

Father had an entire night to regret his offer. He had never drawn a pint and had no idea how to use the card reader for payment. But at three o'clock on the dot, he was at the pub. James looked flustered.

"I'm expecting a delivery. If it arrives while I'm away, make sure to check the number of casks against the invoice. The kitchen is closed until five-thirty."

James and Erika disappeared before Father

could ask them anything.

He was still looking for a piece of paper to write a "cash only" sign when the first customers walked in, a family with small children.

"Can we have the lunch menu?" the father asked wearily.

"Sorry, the kitchen is closed."

The children started to cry.

"Please, just a slice of bread would do," the mother pleaded.

Father was moved to compassion and went to the kitchen to make something for them. He was buttering toast when a van skidded into the rear car park. Oh, no, the delivery. He rushed to serve the toasts.

"Can we have the bill?" the father asked.

Oh, no, the card reader. "A cash donation will do," Father said, before running to the cellar.

Two casks were missing. At first, the driver made shifty excuses, but eventually confessed that the brewery was going through a rough patch. They had laid off so many people that corners were being cut everywhere. He was worried for his job and his family's future. Father offered him a tissue.

By the time Father returned to the bar, some men from his parish, including Belinda's

Declan, were waiting to be served.

After the initial surprise at seeing him behind the counter, they told him how to draw their pints.

"Where are James and Erika?" the men asked him.

"Having an afternoon off."

Everyone had heard about the fracas at the fête. The conversation moved to the troubles of married life. They shared their own experiences and offered each other comfort. Father felt closer to them than he had since he'd taken over the parish.

When James and Erika emerged holding hands and smiling, the men told them they should keep Father working for them.

"We can't afford to pay him as much as God," James, a self-professed atheist, said.

"I'll just come for a drink, then," Father replied. Anything but the scrumpy!

18. THE HOT AIR BALLOON

Nathan climbed off the tractor after a hard day's work at the Jenkins' farm.

"Look!" Katie said, pointing to the sky, which was dotted with hot air balloons of all shapes and colours.

"They must have come for next week's Bristol Balloon Fiesta," Nathan said.

"They're so beautiful."

"Have you entered the draw?"

"Which draw?"

"Tonight, in our parish hall, there will be a draw for a balloon ride for two. It's in aid of the cinema refurbishment fund."

"I'd love to win that! Am I too late to buy a ticket?" she said.

"My mum is selling them. Don't worry, I'll get you one. Let's meet tonight at the parish hall and I'll be there with your ticket."

Nathan ran home but he was disappointed.

"Sorry. I've already returned any unsold

tickets to Father," his mum said.

"Can I buy a ticket at the door?"

"I don't think so."

Nathan ran to the church. Father was praying the vespers so Nathan had to wait. By the time he could speak to Father, it was almost half-past-seven. The lottery draw was at eight.

"Sorry, Nathan. I've returned all the unsold tickets to the Prices. They're the organisers."

It was too late to walk to the Prices' farm, so Nathan ran back home and jumped on his bicycle. Farmer Price was out on the fields and Mrs Price told Nathan how to get to him. The terrain wasn't suitable for Nathan's road bike, so he had to go on foot. By the time he found Farmer Price, it was seven-forty-five. Shouldn't Farmer Price be on his way to attend the draw?

"Sorry, Nathan. I haven't got anything to do with this lottery. It's my wife who's organising it."

Nathan ran back through the fields, jumped over stiles and got to the farmhouse just as Mrs Price was getting into her car.

"Why didn't you tell me you were looking for me? How many tickets would you like?" she asked.

After all the trouble he had been through, it

felt silly to only ask for one ticket, so he bought an entire book. He would give Katie one ticket and keep the rest for himself. Even if the thought of hanging from a balloon in the middle of the sky terrified him, if he landed the winning ticket, he would take Katie with him. So long as he didn't look down from the basket, it might turn out to be a romantic evening.

He made it to the parish hall just in time. He gave Katie her ticket.

"Thank you. I hope it wasn't too much trouble," she said.

"None at all."

As the numbers tumbled inside the drum, Katie reached for his hand and squeezed it. Nathan's heart suddenly beat faster.

Father Okoli pulled a ticket out of the drum. "The winning ticket is...one hundred and twenty-nine!" he announced.

Katie's shoulders slumped. "I haven't won."

Nathan smiled. "But I have, and I'm taking you with me."

Katie didn't smile back. "It's okay, don't worry. You can take someone else."

A lump formed in Nathan's throat: was Katie turning down her favourite thing because she didn't want to be in his company?

"But I thought that you really wanted to go on a hot air balloon."

Katie chuckled. "I didn't: I don't like flames. I only wanted to win so that I could give my ticket to my mum. She's always dreamed of going on a hot air balloon." Her face lit up. "I have an idea: how about you take my mum with you?"

Oh, no. Getting vertigo with Katie's mum in the basket with him would be terribly embarrassing. How could he get out of it without being rude or admitting that he was terrified of heights? "Actually, I'm not so keen on hot air balloons either, but I'd be very happy to give both tickets to your mum and she can take anyone she likes."

"That's so kind of you, thank you. And how about we go along and watch the balloons from the ground?"

"That sounds like a great plan."

Mrs Jenkins accepted Nathan's offer eagerly and invited her husband to go with her. Nathan and Katie watched Mr and Mrs Jenkins soar up into a beautiful sunset, while they sat on a picnic mat enjoying strawberries and cream with their feet firmly on the ground.

19. OUTSIDERS

Belinda looked at the notice on the village board. Watering gardens with hosepipes wasn't allowed for the next ten days, and baths were highly discouraged.

They'd had a dry spring and an even drier summer so far, but what the town councillors were worried about was the extra burden on the water supply caused by the horse trials.

Every year, the Earl of Oldwell held horse trials in the grounds of his enormous estate that stretched all round the village. The event attracted horse lovers from all over the world, causing gridlocks in the road, queues in the shops and exorbitant prices in every B&B and hotel for miles around.

Belinda had done a big grocery shop to avoid the queues once the visitors arrived, and was lugging her shopping home when she spotted her neighbour, Grant, getting into a taxi with a suitcase. What a good idea, to go on holiday while the village was taken by storm.

She was already feeling sorry for herself when she noticed a people carrier, with a car pass for the horse trials stuck on the windscreen, parked in front of Grant's house. Belinda had heard there was money to be made in holiday letting, but the thought of giving her house to strangers had put her off. And now she was the only one left behind to endure their village being overrun by outsiders.

She didn't greet her new neighbours. She tutted when they were loading picnics and children into the car, blocking the pavement, and when a full wash of clothes appeared on their line, she posted the hosepipe ban notice through their letter-box.

But every shopkeeper in the village was very happy. This was the best time of year for local businesses. The pub was full to the brim, the teashop had spilled onto the pavement and the butcher's had started selling hot dogs.

Belinda was going home with a hot dog lunch when she met Reverend Mark.

"Good morning, Belinda. How are you?"

"I'll be happier when the horse trials are over. I don't understand all this fuss."

"Have you been to watch?"

"I would never spend that kind of money on a ticket, even if I had plenty to spare," she said moodily.

"If I manage to get free tickets, would you come with me? I've never been."

Her pride told her to say no, but she was curious.

Mark took her hesitation as a positive response. "Keep tomorrow free and I'll be in touch."

The next day, Mark picked her up early, and they joined the queues for the Oldwell Horse Trials.

Beautifully groomed horses jumped over lakes and hedges, danced in the arenas, galloped through wooded stretches. There were stalls, shops and food vans, pavilions and stages. It was a horsey-themed fairground like nothing she had ever seen before.

Father Okoli was there, too, and seemed to be enjoying himself, talking to the Nigerian team.

At the end of the day, Mark dropped her off home. She thanked him. "You haven't told me yet how you got our passes."

"Come," he said, getting out of the car.

He strode up to Grant's door and rang the bell. The tenants opened the door.

"Belinda, meet my brother, Leo."

Brother? These strangers she had disliked so much were Mark's family?

The man offered her his hand, while his kids ran down the stairs screeching.

"Uncle Mark!"

"Thanks for the pass. We've really enjoyed the show," Mark told Leo, handing him the car pass.

"We needed a rest after the kids fell in one of the lakes. We had to wash all their clothes." Leo sighed.

So they had given Mark and herself their pass, and the washing had been a necessity. Belinda flushed in shame.

"It's hard to keep kids entertained in a house without toys, I guess," Mark said.

"I still have a box of toys from when my boy was little. Would you like to borrow it?" Belinda said.

"Oh, yes, please! Thank you so much," Leo said.

"Not a problem. After all, neighbours must help each other," Belinda said.

20. CAT-HOLIC

Father Okoli looked out of the window of the parish office. The neighbours had just installed a fishpond with a cheerful tinkling fountain, iridescent koi carp and lights that came on at dusk.

But for their cat, it was temptation on a platter. Before the arrival of the pond, the cat used to spend his time keeping Father's hens company, deterring the birds from stealing their seeds. Now the hens had to fend for themselves, while the cat spent his days pawing at the net that covered the pond.

Belinda burst into the parish office. "Sorry I'm late, Father. I met James Loft. Erika has had the baby!"

"Erika was expecting?" He had seen her when she came to clean the church, but had never realised she was pregnant.

Belinda rolled her eyes. "It's a good thing you don't have a wife, Father."

The phone rang. A couple he had never met wanted to be married in the church. The next call was from someone requesting a Confirmation certificate.

"I can't find any records of you having received the Sacrament," Father said.

"I haven't, but can't you write me a certificate anyway?" the person said.

The next caller wanted her children to receive First Holy Communion. "We don't attend church, but I'll send the kids if there are compulsory lessons," the woman said, as if they were dealing with karate classes or violin lessons.

Father sat back in his chair, tired and deflated. "Sometimes I feel like a Sacrament vending machine," he told Belinda.

Just then, there was a knock on the door.

"Come in," he answered.

The door opened and a pram rolled in, followed by Erika and James Loft. Father sprang to his feet.

"Hello! Congratulations!" He rushed to the pram but stopped at a distance, while Belinda peeked right in.

"What a beautiful baby!" she cooed.

"Her name is Bernadette!" Erika said proudly.

It was an unusually religious name for the

daughter of an atheist like James, Father noticed.

"Have a seat. Can I offer you tea?" he said.

"No, thank you. We just wanted to ask you if you could baptise her," Erika said. James nodded.

"Great. Let's put it in the diary!" Father bounced back to the desk, feeling more like an excited puppy than a Sacrament vending machine.

It was hot on the day of the baptism. Despite all church doors and windows being open, Father was sweltering under his vestments. How he would have liked to splash his face with the water of the baptismal font!

The neighbours' cat strutted in, scratched his back against the pews and played with the altar cloth's tassels.

"Do you mind Cat-holic, Father?" Belinda asked.

He gave her a puzzled look.

"That's what we call the cat."

Father smiled. "No, I don't mind him."

Erika and James arrived punctually with the baby, her godparents and all their friends and family, and Father started the ceremony. The gospel reading was the story of the miraculous fish catch.

When it was time for the baptism rites, the

parents, godparents and the baby gathered around the baptismal font. Father dipped his silver shell scoop into the basin.

"I baptise you in the name of..." He stopped. A beautiful koi carp—just like the ones in the neighbours' pond—swam happily in the water.

"A fish!" the baby's godmother cried out.

"It's a miracle!" Erika shouted.

James's eyes widened, colour drained from his face and he reeled. The godfather caught him. Commotion followed.

"Silence," Father requested, trying to avoid pouring the fish on to the baby's head.

James came to and pleaded to be baptised straight after his daughter.

Eventually, the baby was fully baptised, everyone had calmed down and Father looked around for the culprit.

There he was, sitting on a pew, flicking his tail and grinning like the Cheshire Cat.

21. SHAKESPEARE IN THE GARDENS

It had been a very dry summer. Every gardener and farmer was desperate for rain. But now that the rain was finally forecast, the actors of the amateur dramatic society were grumbling.

They were due to perform "Romeo and Juliet" in the gardens of the Catholic church.

"The chance of rain between seven and nine this evening is only fifty per cent," Anne, the society's chair and village butcher, said.

"Well, make sure we finish on time," Grant grumbled.

"We'll finish on time if you don't go off on one of your off-the-cuff monologues," publican James said.

"And you'd better get changed quickly," Grant retorted.

During dress rehearsals, James had taken ages to change from Benvolio into Lady Capulet and had kept everyone waiting.

"I'd like to see you get into a petticoat in less than ten seconds," James quipped.

"It's not James's fault. We're too few for the number of parts we have to play," Rob, Anne's husband, pointed out. He was playing Romeo and also Juliet's maid.

"I guess that other people don't dare join us because they're intimidated by our skills," James said.

"Hear, hear!" Grant agreed heartily. "That's why our shows always sell out!"

"Our shows sell out because people love a picnic in the gardens, and that's why we can't move indoors," Anne reminded him.

That evening they were all ready with their costumes layered in their right order and the props laid out behind the thick yew hedge that served as their backstage. The church gardens were teeming with people, picnic chairs, tables and blankets, but also a few umbrellas discreetly tucked away.

At five to seven, Father Okoli stepped onto the stage. "Thank you for coming tonight. Every penny you donate will go towards the refurbishment of the village's old Electric Picture House. Volunteers will be going round with buckets."

The volunteers shook their buckets.

"We'll start promptly and hope to beat the

rain. Enjoy the show!"

People clapped and the play started.

Romeo and Juliet met, fell in love and Juliet, played by Anne, was just starting the balcony scene when a clap of thunder drowned her words.

"My beloved, we should take this indoors, methinks," Romeo stated. Murmurs of agreement rippled through the audience.

Before she knew what was happening, Romeo had swept her off her feet and carried her indoors. What with the surprise, the commotion and the unfamiliar stage, Anne had completely lost track of where they had got to in the play. Whose line was it?

"What's Montague? It is nor hand, nor foot, nor arm, nor face," Farmer Jenkins' daughter, Katie, called from the front row. But what line came next?

Anne looked at Katie in panic and she continued. "What's in a name? That which we call a rose by any other name would smell as sweet."

Anne's mind was still blank. She nodded at Katie to continue.

When she got to the end of Juliet's monologue and it was Romeo's turn, a boy's voice rose shyly from the back of the hall. "Call me but love, and I'll be new baptized;

henceforth I never will be Romeo." It was Belinda's son, Nathan.

Anne gestured for them to come up on stage. Nathan's cheeks flared up and he glanced at Katie. She nodded and they climbed the steps together.

While they played Romeo and Juliet, Rob and Anne concentrated on finding the props for their other characters, which were now jumbled up in a pile hastily swept up from the garden.

Nathan and Katie played it beautifully, with a hint of shyness that fitted their characters to a tee. At the end of the play, a standing ovation ripped through the parish hall.

"I'm sure I'm not the only one wondering how you knew all your lines?" Anne asked Katie and Nathan.

"I studied this play for my English GCSE," Nathan said.

"I studied it for my drama exam," Katie added.

Anne had an idea. "Would you like to join the society?"

22. A BOOK FOR EVERYONE

When the bishop had given him a third parish to look after, Father Okoli had let go of his dream of studying for a PhD. But there were other dreams in his heart he hadn't given up on.

"What are you writing, Father?" Erika asked him while she dusted the shelves of the parish office with baby Bernadette strapped to her back.

"A book about symbols in the history of salvation."

"Nah, Father, nobody wants to read that. How about 'refugees in the history of salvation'? Much more interesting."

She had come from Bulgaria and he had come from Nigeria, so they both knew what it was like to be an outsider, even though Father was feeling at home in the village now.

"An interesting topic, but it's not what I had in mind."

"How about 'women in the history of salvation'?" Belinda suggested from her desk.

"Plenty of people cleverer than me have written about it."

"Because it's a very important topic. You should write about it, Father," Belinda insisted.

Luckily, the phone rang, putting an end to a conversation that looked set to disappoint everyone.

That evening, when Father went to the pub, James, Erika's husband, poured him a pint.

"Father, I have a much better idea for your book: 'publicans and innkeepers in the gospels'. We are everywhere in the gospels."

James, an atheist, had been rattled by a certain "miracle" at his daughter's christening, and had clearly done a lot of religious reading.

Farmer Jenkins, who was sitting at the bar next to Father, joined in. "Farmers are more important: in the bible there's always someone sowing seeds and reaping harvests somewhere."

"The apostles were fishermen," the fishmonger said. "Father should write a book about fishermen."

"Hear, hear," Rob, the butcher, said in high-street solidarity.

"I wouldn't read any of those," his wife, Anne, said, "but if the book was about marriage, for example…"

"Father's book isn't for people like us to read. It's for priests," Rob said.

"Quite, and that's why Father must decide what it's about," Grant, the local cycling champion, said.

The conversation moved on to the Wacky Races the following weekend, but Rob's words kept ringing in Father's ears. Was he really writing a book that only priests would read?

The next day, the village was abuzz with speculation about Father's book. Everywhere he went, Father was bombarded with suggestions.

Helped by the delicious smells in the bakery, the baker almost managed to persuade Father to write about bread in the gospels.

But when Father got home and opened his laptop to check whether what he was writing was as unappealing as the whole village made it sound, he was instantly in love with his book again. How could he have thought of writing anything else?

Never mind if only a few priests and theologians would read it. There clearly was a book for everyone, and this one was for him.

Still, as he typed, he couldn't forget the way everyone's eyes had sparkled when they had talked about their pet topics. An idea flashed across his mind.

He scribbled a note for the village noticeboard: Writing group every Saturday in the parish hall. No previous experience required. Then he rang everyone who had offered him ideas and invited them personally.

The following Saturday, the parish hall was full. As they all sat round the tables where Father had laid out pens and paper, Bibles and reference books, some of them looked excited, some nervous.

"Well done for making the first step towards writing your books: coming tonight. All your ideas were interesting but I'm not the best person to write them. That person is you, because you are passionate about them. I'll be at hand to answer any questions or point you to the sources for your research. If you want, at the end I'll also help you publish your books."

Everyone clapped and cheered.

23. THE GREAT RACE

August Bank Holiday meant one thing in Moreton-on-the Edge: the Wacky Races. Teams raced home-built push cars down the escarpment on which the village was built.

It was the reverse of the May Bank Holiday Cheese Race, where fit villagers ran uphill with a heavy cheese wheel on their shoulders. The Wacky Races had been dubbed "The Lazy Races", which suited Nathan very well, as he was always last at games. This year his dad and their neighbours on either side, Grant and Mr Barrington, had formed a team and had asked him to drive.

"We've done our bit. Now it's your turn, young man," Grant, who built the car's chassis and controls, said.

Mr Barrington had made the bodywork and painted it in British racing green with a beautiful Union Jack. "Try not to scrape the paintwork. We wouldn't like to see scratches on the photos of the winning car."

Nathan swallowed. What if he didn't win?

His dad patted his shoulder. "You can do it, my boy."

Teams were paired by draw and were going to race each other in a process of elimination.

The presenter shouted into the microphone. "Buckets are going round for your donations towards the refurbishment of our Electric Picture House. Our next race is Firemen versus Primrose Close!"

Oh, no, they had been pitted against the firemen, who were last year's winners!

The firemen struck the bell of their miniature fire engine and squirted water from their toy hosepipe. The spectators cheered. They were everyone's favourites.

Nathan's palms turned clammy. Even if he managed to snatch victory, the crowd would be disappointed.

Was Katie cheering for him or for the firemen? He scanned the crowd. No sign of her. He took out his hearing aid, shoved it into his pocket and put on his helmet.

He felt his dad, Grant and Mr Barrington take hold of the back of the car, ready to give it the strong push that would propel him down the hill. Four beefy firemen got into position behind their car. Three pushers weren't going to cut it against four!

Nathan scanned the crowd in panic. Father Okoli caught his eye, nodded, then walked up to the race director and asked him something. Next thing, Father was behind the car, ready to be the fourth pusher.

The flag went down and Nathan's team gave a mighty shove, but the fire engine lurched out like a Formula One car and was hurtling downhill, spraying water on the ecstatic crowd.

The fire engine was heavier than Nathan's car and accelerated faster. At the first corner, the engine wobbled, drawing gasps from the crowd.

Nathan took the chance to overtake his adversary. At Old Oak Corner, Nathan leaned over the side so much that his elbow rubbed against tarmac, but he managed not to brake. He negotiated one last corner, then saw the chequered flag. He was winning!

Just then, out of the corner of his eye, he saw the fire engine. It overtook him and crossed the finish line a millisecond before his car.

He took off his helmet, wiped his brow and put his hearing aid back in, in time to hear the crowd cheer.

"I'm really sorry," he said to his team.

"What for?" Grant asked.

"Losing, after all the work you've done on the car."

Grant laughed. "I've loved every bit of the work. I would have been gutted if you won and wrecked the car."

"Quite! I don't care whether we win or not. I just like people admiring my paintwork," Mr Barrington said.

Suddenly, a girl ran out of the crowd. Katie!

"Congratulations, Nathan!" she said.

"What for?"

"Haven't you heard? You won! The fire engine went off the road at Old Oak Corner. Spectators helped it back up and pushed it, so the team is disqualified."

Nathan didn't care whether he had won the race or not. Katie had come to watch him. His chest swelled with happiness.

His dad came forward. "Well done, my boy. Now, say goodbye to Katie and push the car back up the hill to race again."

"Remember. Careful of the paintwork," said a smiling Mr Barrington.

24. A WONDERFUL DUNG HEAP

Father Okoli was getting ready to go to St. Mary's primary school to celebrate Mass for the beginning of the new academic year. He was looking forward to it. Being involved in the school was a big component of becoming part of the local community.

He was about to leave the presbytery when the phone rang. It was Farmer Price's wife.

"Father, there's been an accident."

"What? Where?" he asked anxiously.

"I have no idea where. That's the problem. I've lost my wedding ring."

Father heaved a sigh of relief, while Mrs Price continued. "It could be anywhere! I've searched the house top to bottom. I'm really upset, Father, so I'm buying a new one. Will you bless it for me?"

"Of course I will."

Father set off for the school. He'd almost reached the gate when he saw Grant, the village's cycling champion, whizzing down the lane on his electric bike.

He was about to wave when a pheasant jumped off the drystone wall and ran in front of the bicycle.

Grant shouted and swerved. Before Father's eyes, Grant's bicycle rode up the bank and catapulted him over the wall into the field, slap bang in the middle of a steaming pile of manure. On the other side of the field, the children in the school playground gasped. Father vaulted the wall and ran to Grant's side.

"Are you okay, Grant? Can you hear me?"

Grant opened one eye. "The priest! Oh, no, I must be dying!" he thought, and closed his eyes again.

"Is there a first aider?" Father called out to the pupils and teachers in the playground.

Grant opened his eyes again and sniffed. "What's this stench? Am I in hell?"

A group of older children, led by their teacher, arrived with a first aid kit. They must have been rehearsing a school play because they were dressed as angels.

"Goodness, I'm not in hell, I'm in heaven!" Grant cried.

"He's in shock," one of the angel first aiders said.

The pheasant, perched on the drystone wall, watched the scene, cocking its head.

The sound of an engine on the lane announced the arrival of the ambulance. The paramedics checked Grant and confirmed that all was well.

"This manure heap saved your life, and we suspect that your backpack protected your spine."

Grant opened the bag and looked inside with a sigh. It was full of broken pastries from the bakery. "Pheasant pies: my favourites!" He darted a reproachful look at the pheasant that was still watching from the wall.

Grant zipped up the backpack and made to stand up, then held his lower back in pain.

The paramedics immediately checked him. "Aha!" They pulled something out of his back and held it up. "How did your wedding ring end up jammed under your belt?"

"This isn't mine. I've never had a wedding ring." Grant frowned.

"Does this field belong to Farmer Price?" Father asked the teacher.

"Yes."

Father didn't need to hear more. He took out his phone and rang Mrs Price. "We've found your ring!"

"Where was it?"

"It's a long story…"

Farmer Price gave Grant a ride home on his tractor. No-one else wanted to offer a lift to a man covered in manure.

When Mrs Price heard how the ring had been found, she explained that she had lost weight and all her rings were now loose. "It must have slipped off when I was helping my husband with the cows."

"You should take it to the jeweller's to have it tightened," Father suggested.

A few days later, Father met Mrs Price again. "How is your ring?"

She beamed. "Very well. My husband didn't like the idea of having it altered and he bought me an eternity ring to wear above it to hold it in place. So now I have two beautiful rings to remind me of him."

Father smiled. Thank goodness for that dung heap!

25. PRIDE AND PREJUDICE

Belinda picked up her sausages from the butcher's counter. "Thanks, Anne. Have a nice evening."

"I sure will, tonight of all nights!" Anne grinned.

"Is something happening tonight?"

"Don't you know?"

"We've just come back from a week in Cornwall," Belinda explained.

Anne smiled smugly. "They've been shooting a period drama at the grand house in the Oldwell estate. But tonight, they're shooting in the village. They've asked us to stay indoors but we can watch from our windows. Connor Flirt is in the cast!"

Connor Flirt! He was Belinda's favourite actor and the most handsome man on the planet. "Thanks, Anne."

Belinda skipped home and burst into the kitchen. Her husband, Declan, was peeling potatoes.

"You won't believe this: they're shooting a Regency romance in the village tonight with Connor Flirt!"

"Katie and her friends were talking about him," Nathan said with a hint of annoyance as he walked in.

"Who?" Declan asked.

"An actor every woman in the village is crazy about," Nathan scoffed.

"Not me," Belinda said. But at seven on the dot, she was at her window, ready to watch the action.

It seemed every curtain on the street was twitching when, suddenly, carriages and horses mounted by men in Regency clothes rushed through the street. And there he was, handsome as ever: Connor Flirt. Belinda's heart did a little somersault.

That night, Belinda dreamed that her car broke down in the lanes and the AA sent Connor Flirt to take her home on his horse.

All the next day at work, she was distracted. Father had to ask her twice where the parish stamp was. After a long search, they discovered that she had absentmindedly put it in her handbag.

"Are you feeling all right?" he asked.

"Very well." She was too embarrassed to

tell him that she was distracted by thoughts of Connor Flirt playing Mr Darcy.

At four-thirty, on her way home, she popped into the butcher's again.

"Belinda, did you hear?" Anne was wild-eyed.

"Hear what?"

"Connor Flirt is stuck in a ditch with his horse, on the Oldwell estate. Farmer Jenkins and all the men of the village have gone to rescue them. Your Declan is there, too, trying to talk sense into the horse."

Belinda jumped into her car and drove to the Oldwell estate.

The whole village was there: Farmer Jenkins with his tractor, Anne's husband, Rob, the village butcher and also the first aider, and even Father.

Declan was patting the twitchy horse and talking into its ear like Robert Redford in "The Horse Whisperer". Declan was bald and would never wear tight jeans, but there was a certain similarity.

"What's happened?" Belinda asked Rob.

"Mr. Darcy and his horse failed to navigate a ha-ha. The camera crew who tried to rescue them in their van have also got stuck in the ditch. Farmer Jenkins is pulling the van out with his tractors, Rob is checking the actor for injuries and your husband is dealing with the horse."

As if he had felt her gaze on him, Declan looked up and smiled at her. Belinda's heart leaped. Then Declan mounted the horse and guided it out of the ha-ha with skill.

A woman from the crew approached him. Suddenly, Belinda felt something she hadn't experienced in ages: jealousy. She marched up to them and put a possessive hand on her husband's leg.

"…we really need to wrap up this scene tonight. The horse clearly likes you and you have a similar build to Connor. Would you be his double for this scene? All you have to do is wear Mr Darcy's costume and ride the horse over the ha-ha."

"If my wife doesn't object." He smiled at her.

"Yes, of course, yes, yes," Belinda said, flustered. Her own Declan was Connor Flirt's body double!

Make-up and costume artists fussed over Declan to get him ready and, as the sun sank languidly behind the grand house, Belinda admired her very own Mr Darcy as he jumped elegantly over the ha-ha.

26. RUBBISH COLLECTION DAY

Father Okoli woke up in a panic: he hadn't put the bins out before bed. He had forgotten bin day two weeks in a row. If he missed it again, his bins would overflow.

He clambered out of bed, slipped into his dressing-gown and traipsed out of the back door. A flash of orange darted in front of him. The fox!

Since Father had caught the animal almost inside his chicken coop, the two of them were sworn enemies.

Father had got into the habit of counting his hens every morning.

He grabbed a torch and shone it onto the henhouse. The fox was digging under the fence.

"Be off!" Father called out and stomped down the path. He followed the animal with his torch as it jumped the wall and disappeared into the woods over the far side of the field.

Just as Father was about to turn away, the beam of his torch intercepted a car and a trailer parked in the field. Men were rounding up the cows.

Why was Farmer Price moving his herd before dawn? Father pointed his torch again. The car didn't look like Farmer Price's car. Maybe the fox wasn't the only one stealing livestock! Anger mounted inside him. Back home in Nigeria, he had seen the damage that cattle rustling did to the victims' livelihoods.

He was on his own and the farmhouse was a long way away. The rustlers might have driven off by the time he returned with help or the police, especially as he had alerted them of his presence with the torch. The best thing he could do was block the gate.

Still in his dressing gown and slippers, Father grabbed his mobile phone, jumped into his car and drove up the lane. He parked across the gate to the field just as the rustlers slammed the trailer's door shut. The cows mooed plaintively inside.

Seeing that their only escape route was blocked, the rustlers abandoned the trailer and the car and ran to the same woods where the fox had disappeared.

Father got out of the car, photographed the

vehicle's number plate and rang the police.

Meanwhile, the mooing grew louder. Father opened the trailer and released the cows. He didn't have Farmer Price's number so he would have to go to the farmhouse. He thought about driving up there, but he didn't want to risk the rustlers returning and driving off. So he left his car in front of the gate and walked.

By the time he got to the farmhouse, the sky was glowing pink and the lights in the house were on.

Farmer Price opened the door fully dressed and ready to start his day's work. He took in Father's dressing-gown and slippers. "Hello, Father. Is everything okay?"

No sooner had Father finished telling him what had happened, than the man was in his car, with the engine on. "Let's go, Father!"

They barrelled down the lane but came to a sudden stop a hundred yards before the field's gate. Farmer Price leaped out of the car to investigate.

"Your car is blocking the lane, Father," Farmer Price reported.

In his haste to stop the thieves, Father had done a handbrake parking like a police car in an action movie. As a result, the recycling lorry couldn't get through.

Oh no! His bins were still in the shed!

With the lorry blocking the lane, also the police car, the milk lorry, the milk float and the post van were stuck, together with the nurse returning from her night shift at the hospital in the city.

Father felt less embarrassed about running down the lane in his dressing-gown than about getting into the car that had held up all these busy and important people.

As he drove off, the recycling lorry trundled behind him. Luckily, it turned into another road and Father had just enough time to put his bins out.

The rustlers were caught and their car and trailer—which were stolen—were returned to their owners.

From then on, every morning after counting his hens, Father counted Farmer Price's cows, too.

27. PLENTY OF SPACE IN THE COUNTRYSIDE

Every morning on her way to work, Belinda walked past the Old Dairy.

It was a beautiful barn conversion, spacious enough for a family, but the For Sale sign had been on the front lawn for months. It was far too expensive.

Belinda had seen the price in the estate agent's window. Nobody in the village could afford it and certainly not her.

But today the sign read Sold. Who had bought it?

A swanky Audi she'd not seen in the village before was parked in the drive. The owners must be rich folks from the city. These people bought up houses in the countryside as second homes, which lay empty most of the year, and caused house prices to balloon out of locals' reach. Soon, they would run out of space in the countryside.

When she arrived at the parish office, Belinda was in a stinking mood.

Father was at the door with his bag. "Hi, Belinda. I'm going to bless a home. I should be back before ten o'clock as it's only down the road: the Old Dairy."

The very house! "Who bought it?"

"A couple from London. Mr and Mrs Campbell. I'll be welcoming them to our parish." Father smiled.

Belinda stiffened. "I'm fed up with city folks buying up all our houses! Where are our children going to set up home?"

Father raised an eyebrow. "I doubt your Nathan will have housing issues if he has his heart set on Farmer Jenkins' daughter."

"It's not just about my Nathan. The village will die if all the houses become second homes and lie empty most of the year."

"Then I'll try to persuade Mr and Mrs Campbell to move to the village permanently," Father said good-naturedly.

Belinda would have rather he persuaded them to leave permanently, but she chased the thought away. "Sorry, Father. I'm not good at dealing with change."

Father smiled. "I understand, and I know what it's like to be the new arrival."

Father wasn't back by ten o'clock as he had

promised, or by lunchtime.

As soon as Belinda imagined the Campbells as murderous priest-nappers, she realised it was much more likely that they had invited him for lunch. Unfortunately, she hated the second possibility as much as the first. How dare the new arrivals hog her favourite priest?

She locked up the parish office and went home. Unusually, her husband was there.

"What a nice surprise. How come you're not having lunch at work?" she asked him.

He looked uneasy. "I've been to the shops to buy you a birthday present, but I couldn't think of anything you might like. So I gave up and came home for lunch."

That thought went a long way to improving her mood.

When she got back to the parish office, Father was at his desk.

"The Campbells invited me to stay for lunch. They are really nice people and the Old Dairy isn't going to be their second home. They have taken early retirement and are going to open a pottery studio and school in their home. Look." He pulled a beautiful terracotta Christmas crib out of a box. "They've given it to the church."

"It's beautiful," Belinda admitted.

On the way home from work, Belinda

walked past the Old Diary. The owners were drinking tea in the garden and greeted her. Belinda introduced herself. "Thank you for the crib. It's the most beautiful I've ever seen," she said.

"Thank you. Can we offer you a cup of tea?"

Belinda stayed for tea and was even given a tour of the pottery workshop.

"I know what I'd like for my birthday," she told Declan that evening.

And that was how Belinda became the first student of the village's new pottery school.

When she went to work the day after her lesson, Father asked how it was.

"I loved it! Declan is putting up a shed in our garden for my studio."

"Do you have space for that?" Father asked.

"Oh, yes. There's plenty of space here in the countryside." She smiled.

28. THE HARVEST DECORATIONS

"Father, Fiona keeps asking me when we're having the harvest celebration," Belinda told Father. "The flower ladies need to know so they can order the flowers and decorations."

Father sighed. Fiona had asked him many times. "I don't know yet. We'll do it as soon as the last farmer has got his harvest in."

Belinda's lips thinned. "In the past, we've always set a date and stuck to it."

"Farmer Jenkins's wheat is still out. We can't go ahead without him."

"He isn't even a Catholic."

"Does it matter? Do we bake bread only with wheat from Catholic farms?"

"Your other two parishes have already celebrated the harvest. Why have you let them and not us?"

Father sighed again. "Is the problem just the church decoration?"

"Yes, but it's not 'just'. The flower ladies

put a lot of effort and time in and the parish spends a good deal of money on it."

"Maybe we should spend time, effort and money on more important things."

"I'm warning you, Father: you're going to upset the flower ladies."

A couple of months ago, Belinda's words would have deterred him, but not now. He felt loved enough by his parish to take risks. "I know what we'll do! Please tell Fiona and the flower ladies that all I need from them is that they keep themselves free to help half an hour before Mass every week until we have the celebration."

By Saturday evening, Father Jenkins's spring wheat was all in and Father made his phone calls.

The next morning, Fiona and the other flower ladies were at the church early. Two cars parked outside and two men started unloading flowers, bread and baskets of produce.

"Wow, Father! Where did you buy all this?" Fiona asked.

"I asked my other parishes, who had their harvest celebrations last week, if they could share it. All we have to do is lay it out inside the church."

Father smiled, but Fiona didn't smile back.

Oh, well, she was probably just overcome by the surprise. "I'd better get ready for Mass. I'll leave you to it."

When Mass started, he walked down the aisle and saw the church bursting with sunflowers, ears of corn and golden loaves. He didn't see the frowns of the flower ladies, but at the end of the celebration, Belinda accosted him.

"You should have a word with the flower ladies. They are rather upset."

What could they be upset about? He had saved them effort and time.

"They're in the parish hall," Belinda said.

As soon as Father stepped into the hall, the group of ladies fell silent.

"I'm sorry if I caused offence. I thought I was doing something good," Father said candidly.

Fiona stared at him. "Celebrating the harvest with... recycled flowers? How can we celebrate our own abundance if we beg from other parishes?"

"But we got the flowers of two parishes. Double what we would have bought for ourselves."

"But why be so stingy as to beg from others?"

"So that we can send the money we've

saved to the homeless shelter in Bristol," Father said.

"Ah." Fiona's frown slowly softened. "Will you let the other parishes know how we're using the money? We don't want them to think that we are, um… scroungers."

"No problem."

Peace was made before the hall filled with the other parishioners having tea and coffee. Farmer Jenkins and his family popped round, too, and thanked him.

When he was on his own, Belinda approached him. "Well? How did it go?"

Father looked at the water jug on the table. "Today I learned it takes more humility to be a water pipe than a water jug. If you are a jug, you can only give a small amount of stale water. But if you are a pipe, you can give endless amounts of fresh water. To be a pipe, you have to receive all the time before you can give. Sometimes receiving is harder than giving."

"Indeed."

29. THE MOP FAIR

Now that Farmer Jenkins's harvest was in, Nathan's summer job at the farm had come to an end.

He had got used to seeing Katie every day as they worked alongside each other, but he no longer had a reason to see her. Desperation gave him the courage and the mop fair provided the opportunity—so he asked her out on a date. She readily agreed.

On the day of the date, he put on clean jeans and a clean T-shirt, sprayed enough deodorant to make himself dizzy, and set off.

Tonight, he would ask Katie to be his girlfriend.

He hadn't even got to the village green when the racket of the rides became so loud that he had to turn down his hearing aid. Perhaps this wasn't the best venue for a romantic evening.

Katie was already there. She smiled and his

heart did a somersault. Katie suggested they went on the teacups ride. They were about to climb on when a child's voice called them. It was one of Katie's cousins.

"Will you take me on the ride?" the little girl asked.

"Of course." Katie helped the child in and sat her between herself and Nathan. No romantic ride after all. Never mind. They had the whole evening ahead.

Next, Nathan suggested the bumper cars. Katie's cousin was too young for that ride, so he would have Katie all for himself.

Their fingers brushed on the car's steering wheel and Katie smiled at him. He gathered enough courage to steer the car to a quiet spot and start the speech he had prepared. "Katie, I have something to tell you—"

Bump! Someone hit them from behind. Nathan whipped round.

"Sorry. I got shunted myself." It was Father Okoli, and he wasn't alone. The entire Churches Together committee, including Nathan's own mother, was there! This was the problem with living in a village: you never got any privacy.

"Shall we find a different ride?" Katie suggested.

As soon as they had left the bumper cars,

someone called behind them. "Hello, Nathan!"

His neighbour, Grant, was waving a bunch of tickets. "Are you coming to the grand opening of our new Electric Picture House?"

"Sure!" Katie said.

The village had pulled together to raise funds to reopen the old cinema, and Nathan was sure that the whole village would be attending the opening. It wouldn't be a romantic evening, but he treasured any time he and Katie could spend together, so he eagerly bought two tickets.

A group of Katie's friends stopped her and asked her if she was coming to the cinema, too. "See you there!" they told her.

Everyone liked Katie. He had fallen in love with a popular girl and he had to get used to sharing her with all the other people that loved her, too.

"Let's take the Ferris wheel!" Katie suggested.

Oh, no. He hated that ride. The last time he had been on it, he had thrown up. But he didn't want to spoil Katie's fun.

The queue was very long so Nathan had time to get goosebumps watching the gondolas rise. By the time they reached the front of the queue, he felt queasy.

If he got onto the wheel, he was sure to be sick. But how could he let Katie down after they had queued for so long?

Just as they were about to get onto the gondola, Katie's little cousin popped out from the crowd.

"Will you take me with you? Mum and Dad don't want to queue," the girl pleaded.

Oh, no. If he was going to be sick, Katie's entire family would hear of it.

"I'm sorry, but the gondolas only have space for two people," Katie said.

The little girl looked disappointed.

"Why don't you two go together and I'll wait here?" Nathan offered.

"That wouldn't be fair..." Katie said.

"I don't mind." He tried his best not to look too relieved, especially as Katie looked a little disappointed.

In the end, the attendant hurried them, and Katie took her cousin on the ride. Nathan happily waited for them down on the ground.

Maybe living in a village, surrounded by family and friends, wasn't such a bad thing.

30. THE LAST VOTE

"I'm going to the committee meeting," Belinda called from the hall.

After years of fund-raising and refurbishment, the old cinema was ready to open its doors again after fifty years.

Her husband, Declan, popped his head out of the kitchen. "Have fun, dear."

"We will. We're deciding on the movies to show."

"Mum, make sure that they include the new 007!" Nathan shouted from upstairs.

Declan shook his head. "Those films are boring. There's a much better movie—"

"I'm sorry to disappoint you both, but I don't think that I'll have power to decide. I'm sure Grant will already have a list. At most, we'll be asked to vote on a shortlist."

Grant, their neighbour, had been the driving force behind the whole project. In his teens, he had been assistant projectionist until the Electric Picture House was ravaged by fire. Reopening the cinema was his brainchild.

"Can you suggest they screen a romantic movie on the opening night?" Nathan asked sheepishly, still from his bedroom.

Belinda and Declan looked at each other and smiled. Their son's sudden change of heart must be to do with a certain girl he might be taking to the cinema.

"I'll do what I can."

When Belinda got to the village hall, Grant had already drawn a full plan of all movies to be screened for the next six months. All he wanted from the committee was the go-ahead.

"I thought we'd be choosing the films today," James, the pub landlord, said. Others nodded.

"What's wrong with my list?" Grant asked, piqued.

"There's nothing wrong, but each of us should be given the chance to suggest a movie," James replied.

"All right. Let's hear your suggestions."

"I hate movies full of gore and dead people," someone said.

"I hate movies without blood or lives in jeopardy," Rob, the butcher, replied.

"I only like them if people are risking their lives for love," his wife, Anne, said.

Just then, Father Okoli rushed in and took a seat. "Sorry I'm late."

"Nothing's more touching than someone ready to die for the people he loves," Anne continued.

"A movie about Jesus! What a great idea!" Father exclaimed.

Grant groaned. "I thought this was going to be a quick meeting. Let's put all your suggestions to the vote."

Action movies, dramas and thrillers were put forward with romances, comedies and animations, but there wasn't enough space on the schedule to satisfy everyone.

Eventually, the screening list was agreed, but which movie should be screened on the opening night? Disagreements flared up again.

"Right. Everyone has one vote," Grant decided.

One by one, everyone voted for the movie they had put forward, and in the end it was a tie.

"Someone hasn't voted," Father pointed out.

"Who hasn't voted yet?" Grant asked the room.

Belinda put up her hand. She didn't want to be the tie-breaker. She hadn't suggested any movie because she couldn't bear the responsibility.

Lots of people had worked hard to reopen this cinema. So many village events had been devoted to fund-raising for the cause. The first movie to be screened at the New Electric Picture House would go down in village history and everyone would know that she'd cast the deciding vote.

Suddenly, she remembered her son's request. He needed a romantic movie to woo his girl. Motherly love swelled in her chest and trumped every fear. "I vote for 'Love at Dawn'."

Some people cheered, others grumbled, but she didn't care. Nathan would be happy.

When she got home, she found him waiting by the door. "Which movie did you choose for opening night?"

"It wasn't up to her to decide," Declan reminded him.

Belinda smiled. "I was wrong. Actually, it was entirely up to me."

31. THE NEW ELECTRIC PICTURE HOUSE

It had taken a lot of fund-raising and effort, but the day had finally arrived. The Electric Picture House was opening its doors again after fifty years.

The whole village was there for the grand event. Father Okoli felt a frisson of excitement. It was such a privilege to be there. Time had flown since his arrival in the parish and now he felt as much a part of the village as anyone.

"Hello, Father," Carlos, the barber, greeted him. He was hand-in-hand with the widow Father had met on his first visit to Carlos's shop. She and her son were newcomers, too. It looked like they would be staying for a long time.

Someone waved at Father from a car. Nathan was at the wheel! He must have passed his test. Katie Jenkins was in the passenger seat. Father waved back at them.

Grant, the man who had dreamed of this day more than anyone, was standing at the door next to a lady who looked a lot like him.

"Welcome, Father. This my sister, Joanna. She's the one who hosts me when I let my house for the horse trials."

Joanna smiled at him.

Inside, James, the pub landlord, and his wife Erika were giving out ice-cream. The cinema had been refurbished beautifully. The chairs were upholstered in red velvet and the projection booth was fitted with the latest digital technologies.

Father took his seat behind Nathan and Katie just as Grant went up on stage and thanked everyone for their support. Then he called every committee member to stand up for a round of applause. Father was one of them and everyone clapped so enthusiastically that he felt his cheeks turn hot.

"If you'd like a movie to be included in the screening programme, write it down and put it in the box by the entrance," Grant finished.

Then the hall darkened and the screen lit up. Highlights of the village's Wacky Races appeared, followed by the fête and other fund-raising events that had allowed this day to happen.

In a clip of the village cheese race, Father saw himself scrambling up the hill with the huge cheese wheel on his back. He had really struggled, until he had seen the fox jump the presbytery's wall, heading for his hens.

Suddenly, a thought chilled him. He'd forgotten to lock up his hens!

He sprinted out of the cinema and ran home. A flash of orange on the wall. Oh, no—the fox had got there before him.

He tried to channel his inner St Francis of Assisi to prepare himself for hen carnage...

But his hens were happily scratching about, while the fox peacefully watched them from the wall. Father and the fox studied each other, then Father smiled. It was silly of him to hate the animal: it, too, needed to eat.

The animal leaped off the wall and disappeared. Father felt like St Francis taming the wolf of Gubbio. Still, just in case, he locked the hens in before returning to the cinema.

They were now showing a romantic movie. In the row behind him, Belinda was teary-eyed and Anne and Rob were holding hands, while in the row in front of him sat Nathan and Katie.

Father felt a little like a gooseberry, especially when Katie rested her head on

Nathan's shoulder.

Father watched Nathan try to circle Katie's shoulders, but his arm was trapped under the armrest. The only way to set it free was if he shook Katie off. Father watched the boy try for a second time and his heart went out to him.

Father reached out in front of him and discreetly pulled the armrest down. Finally, Nathan put his arm around Katie's shoulders.

Father smiled. He didn't need to watch the rest of the movie. He had already seen happy endings or happy-for-now in the people around him.

He certainly couldn't complain. He was managing three parishes without too much drama, he still had all his hens and his book was slowly developing.

He felt completely at home in Moreton-on-the-Edge. He had found a new family.

The End

Other books by Stefania Hartley:

Drive Me Crazy:

"Cohabitation is tribulation" goes an Italian saying, and after more than fifty years of married life, Tanino and Melina know a thing or two about the challenges of living together. Follow their antics as they compete to give their grandchild the best birthday present, struggle to lose some extra weight, and try to make it to their godchild's christening on time in this collection of twelve short stories dedicated entirely to the much-loved Sicilian couple from the pages of The People's Friend magazine.

Stars Are Silver:

Is it too late for Melina to learn to drive? Is Don Pericle's vow never to fall in love again still valid after fifty years? Will a falling piano squash Filomena or just shake up her heart? Why does the mother of the bride ask Don Pericle to cancel the wedding?

Fresh from the Sea:

Will Gnà Peppina give her customers what they need, even if it's more than food? What pleasures can a man indulge in after his wife has put him on a draconian diet? Who will be able to cook dinner for the family with five euros?

Confetti and Lemon Blossom:

For Don Pericle, wedding organising is a calling, not just a career. Deep in the Sicilian countryside, between rose gardens and trellised balconies, up marble staircases and across damasked ballrooms, these charming stories unfold: stories of star-crossed love, of comedic misunderstandings and of deep friendships, of love triumphing in the face of adversity.

A Slip of the Tongue:

Will Melina regret faking to be sick to avoid her chores? Can Don Pericle organise a wedding for a groom who doesn't know? Who has stolen the marble pisces from the cathedral's floor?

What's Yours is Mine:

Can Melina give away her husband's possessions because they've always said that 'what's mine is yours and what's yours is mine'? Will the 'Sleep Doctor' deliver on his promises? How will the young Sicilian duke, Pericle, help his friend get married?

A Season of Goodwill:
How far should Viviana's family go to avoid being thirteen at the table? Should Melina and Tanino attend a New Year's party hosted by Melina's old flame? Why do Don Pericle's clients want a Christmas wedding at all costs?

The Italian Fake Date:
When Alice Baker discovers that she's been adopted, she knows she won't have peace until she's found her Italian birth mother. But all she has is a letter written twenty-five years ago and an old address.

Jaded about love and unable to forgive his ex-fiancée and his brother, Paolo Rondino is struggling to find inspiration for a sculpture that will make or break his career. Hoping that a trip home will help him find his muse again, he decides to return to Italy, even if this means confronting the two people who betrayed him.

Alice and Paolo strike a deal: he will help her find her birth mother and she will pretend to be his girlfriend to please his mother. It looks like the perfect exchange, until real feelings start to grow…

ABOUT THE AUTHOR

Also known as The Sicilian Mama, Stefania was born in Sicily and immediately started growing, but not very much.

She left her sunny island after falling head over heels in love with an Englishman, and now she lives in the UK with her husband and their three children.

Having finally learnt English, she's enjoying it so much that she now writes short stories and romance novels. Her short stories have been longlisted for the Mogford Prize for Food and Drink Writing, commended by the Society of Medical Authors, and won other prizes.

If you have enjoyed these stories, please

consider leaving a review on Amazon or Goodreads.

If you want to hear when she's releasing a new book, sign up for the newsletter at:
www.stefaniahartley.com/subscribe
You'll also receive an exclusive short story.

Printed in Great Britain
by Amazon

24226983R00076